Going Nowhere

Rebecca Berrett

Houghton Mifflin Company • Boston

Atlanta • Dallas • Geneva, Illinois • Palo Alto • Princeton

Hello Mom.

Good morning
Nick!

2

Where are we going today Mom?
Nowhere, Nick.
Nowhere today.

Nowhere. Mmm . . .
I wonder where
Nowhere is?
Is it near Grandpa's
house, or at the beach?

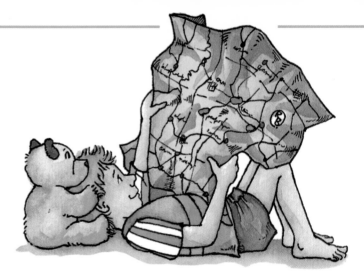

Maybe it's near
a farm.

Who would like to come to
Nowhere with me?
We'll have great fun.

What will we do when we get there?

Will we swim under the waves?

Or search for shells in the sand?

Will we climb mountain slopes?

Or hike through green forests?

We might spend the night
at Nowhere.

10

If we do, Mom will
need these things.

I'll need these things.

How will I
carry everything?

Nick, you look like you're
packed to go somewhere.

I'd like to come with you, Nick.

Where are you going?

Nowhere, Mom.
Nowhere!